A COURSE IN MAGIC

Fantasy and Horror Classics

By

E. NESBIT

First published in 1901

British Library Cataloguing-in-Publication Data
A catalogue record for this book is available
from the British Library

CONTENTS

E. Nesbit 5

FORTUNATUS REX & CO. 7

E. NESBIT

Edith Nesbit was born in Kennington, Surrey in 1858. Her family moved around constantly during her youth, living variously in Brighton, Buckinghamshire, France, Spain and Germany, before settling for three years in Halstead in north-west Kent, a location which later inspired her well-known novel, *The Railway Children*. In 1880, Nesbit married Hubert Bland, and her writing talents – which had been in evidence during her teens – were quickly needed to bring in extra money.

Over the course of her life, Nesbit would go on to publish approximately 40 books for children, including novels, collections of stories and picture books. Among her best-known works are *The Story of the Treasure Seekers* (1898), *The Wouldbegoods* (1899) and *The Railway Children* (1906). Nesbit is regarded by many critics as the first truly 'modern' children's writer, in that she replaced the fantastical worlds utilised by authors such as Lewis Carroll with real-life settings marked by the occasional intrusion of magic. In this, Nesbit is seen as a precursor to writers such as J. K. Rowling and C. S. Lewis. Nesbit was also a lifelong socialist; in 1884 she was among the founding members of the influential Fabian Society. For much of her adult life she was an active lecturer and prolific writer on socialism.

Having suffered from lung cancer for some years, Nesbit died in 1924 at New Romney, Kent, aged 65.

FORTUNATUS REX & CO.

THERE was once a lady who found herself in middle life with but a slight income. Knowing herself to be insufficiently educated to be able to practise any other trade or calling, she of course decided, without hesitation, to enter the profession of teaching. She opened a very select Boarding School for Young Ladies. The highest references were given and required. And in order to keep her school as select as possible, Miss Fitzroy Robinson had a brass plate fastened on to the door, with an inscription in small polite lettering. (You have, of course, heard of the "polite letters." Well, it was with these that Miss Fitzroy Robinson's door-plate was engraved.)

"SELECT BOARDING ESTABLISHMENT FOR THE
DAUGHTERS OF RESPECTABLE MONARCHS."

A great many kings who were not at all respectable would have given their royal ears to be allowed to send their daughters to this school, but Miss Fitzroy Robinson was very firm about references, and the consequence was that all the really high-class kings were only too pleased to be permitted to pay ten thousand pounds a year for their daughters' education. And so Miss Fitzroy Robinson was able to lay aside a few pounds as a provision for her old age. And all the money she saved was invested in land.

Only one monarch refused to send his daughter to Miss Fitzroy Robinson, on the ground that so cheap a school could not be a really select one, and it was found out afterwards that his references were not at all satisfactory.

There were only six boarders, and of course the best masters were engaged to teach the royal pupils everything which their parents wished them to learn, and as the girls were never asked to do lessons except when they felt quite inclined, they all said it was the nicest school in the world, and cried at the very thought of being taken away. Thus it happened that the six pupils were quite grown up and were just becoming parlour boarders when events began to occur. Princess Daisy, the daughter of King Fortunatus, the ruling sovereign, was the only little girl in the school.

Now it was when she had been at school about a year, that a ring came at the front door-bell, and the maid-servant came to the schoolroom with a visiting card held in the corner of her apron—for her hands were wet because it was washing-day.

"A gentleman to see you, Miss," she said; and Miss Fitzroy Robinson was quite fluttered because she thought it might be a respectable monarch, with a daughter who wanted teaching.

But when she looked at the card she left off fluttering, and said, "Dear me!" under her breath, because she was very genteel. If she had been vulgar like some of us she would have said "Bother!" and if she had been more vulgar than, I hope, any of us are, she might have said "Drat the man!" The card was large and shiny and had gold letters on it. Miss Fitzroy Robinson read:—

Chevalier Doloro De Lara
Professor of Magic (white) and the Black Art.
Pupils instructed at their own residences.
No extras.
Special terms for Schools. Evening Parties attended.

Miss Fitzroy Robinson laid down her book—she never taught without a book—smoothed her yellow cap and her grey curls and went into the front parlour to see her visitor. He bowed low at sight of her. He was very tall and hungry-looking, with black eyes, and an indescribable mouth.

"It is indeed a pleasure," said he, smiling so as to show every one of his thirty-two teeth—a very polite, but very difficult thing to do—"it is indeed a pleasure to meet once more my old pupil."

"The pleasure is mutual, I am sure," said Miss Fitzroy Robinson. If it is sometimes impossible to be polite and truthful at the same moment, that is not my fault, nor Miss Fitzroy Robinson's.

"I have been travelling about," said the Professor, still smiling immeasurably, "increasing my stock of wisdom. Ah, dear lady—we live and learn, do we not? And now I am really a far more competent teacher than when I had the honour of instructing you. May I hope for an engagement as Professor in your Academy?"

"I have not yet been able to arrange for a regular course of Magic," said the schoolmistress; "it is a subject in which parents, especially royal ones, take but too little interest."

"It was your favourite study," said the professor.

"Yes—but—well, no doubt some day——"

"But I want an engagement *now*," said he, looking hungrier than ever; "a thousand pounds for thirteen lessons—to *you*, dear lady."

"It's quite impossible," said she, and she spoke firmly, for she knew from history how dangerous it is for a Magician to be allowed anywhere near a princess. Some harm almost always comes of it.

"Oh, very well!" said the Professor.

"You see my pupils are all princesses," she went on, "they don't require the use of magic, they can get all they want without it."

"Then it's 'No'?" said he.

"It's 'No thank you kindly,'" said she.

Then, before she could stop him, he sprang past her out at the door, and she heard his boots on the oilcloth of the passage. She flew after him just in time to have the schoolroom door slammed and locked in her face.

"Well, I never!" said Miss Fitzroy Robinson. She hastened to the top of the house and hurried down the schoolroom chimney, which had been made with steps, in case of fire or other emergency. She stepped out of the grate on to the schoolroom hearthrug just one second too late. The seven Princesses were all gone, and the Professor of Magic stood alone among the inkstained desks, smiling the largest smile Miss Fitzroy Robinson had seen yet.

"Oh, you naughty, bad, wicked man, you!" said she, shaking the school ruler at him.

* * * * *

The next day was Saturday, and the King of the country called as usual to take his daughter Daisy out to spend her half holiday. The servant who opened the door had a coarse apron on and cinders in her hair, and the King thought it was sackcloth and ashes, and said so a little anxiously, but the girl said, "No, I've only been a-doing of the kitchen range—though, for the matter of that—but you'd best see missus herself."

So the King was shown into the best parlour where the tasteful wax-flowers were, and the antimacassars and water-colour drawings executed by the pupils, and the wool mats which Miss Fitzroy Robinson's bed-ridden aunt made so beautifully. A delightful parlour full of the traces of the refining touch of a woman's hand.

Miss Fitzroy Robinson came in slowly and sadly. Her gown was neatly made of sack-cloth—with an ingenious trimming of small cinders sewn on gold braid—and some larger-sized cinders dangled by silken threads from the edge of her lace cap.

The King saw at once that she was annoyed about something. "I hope I'm not too early," said he.

"Your Majesty," she answered, "not at all. You are always punctual, as stated in your references. Something has happened. I will not aggravate your misfortunes by breaking them to you. Your daughter Daisy, the pride and treasure of our little circle, has disappeared. Her six royal companions are with her. For the present all are safe, but at the moment I am unable to lay my hand on any one of the seven."

The King sat down heavily on part of the handsome walnut and rep suite (ladies' and gentlemen's easy-chairs, couch and six occasional chairs) and gasped miserably. He could not find words. But the schoolmistress had written down what she was going to say on a slate and learned it off by heart, so she was able to go on fluently.

"Your Majesty, I am not wholly to blame—hang me if I am—I mean hang me if you must; but first allow me to have the honour of offering to you one or two explanatory remarks."

With this she sat down and told him the whole story of the Professor's visit, only stopping exactly where I stopped when I was telling it to you just now.

The King listened, plucking nervously at the fringe of a purple and crimson antimacassar.

"I never *was* satisfied with the Professor's methods," said Miss Fitzroy Robinson sadly; "and I always had my doubts as to his moral character, doubts now set at rest for ever. After concluding my course of instruction with him some years ago I took a series of lessons from a far more efficient master, and thanks to those lessons, which were, I may mention, extremely costly, I was mercifully enabled to put a spoke in the wheel of the unprincipled ruffian——"

"Did you save the Princesses?" cried the King.

"No; but I can if your Majesty and the other parents will leave the matter entirely in my hands."

"It's rather a serious matter," said the King; "my poor little Daisy——"

"I would ask you," said the schoolmistress with dignity, "not to attach too much importance to this event. Of course it is regrettable, but unpleasant accidents occur in all schools, and the consequences of them can usually be averted by the exercise of tact and judgment."

"I ought to hang you, you know," said the King doubtfully.

"No doubt," said Miss Fitzroy Robinson, "and if you do you'll never see your Daisy again. Your duty as a parent—yes—and your duty to me—conflicting duties are very painful things."

"But can I trust you?"

"I may remind you," said she, drawing herself up so that the cinders rattled again, "that we exchanged satisfactory references at the commencement of our business relations."

The King rose. "Well, Miss Fitzroy Robinson," he said, "I have been entirely satisfied with Daisy's progress since she has been in your charge, and I feel I cannot do better than leave this matter entirely in your able hands."

The schoolmistress made him a curtsey, and he went back to his marble palace a broken-hearted monarch, with his crown all on one side and his poor, dear nose red with weeping.

The select boarding establishment was shut up.

Time went on and no news came of the lost Princesses.

The King found but little comfort in the fact that his other child, Prince Denis, was still spared to him. Denis was all very well and a nice little boy in his way, but a boy is not a girl.

The Queen was much more broken-hearted than the King, but of course she had the housekeeping to see to and the making of the pickles and preserves and the young Prince's stockings to knit, so she had not much time for weeping, and after a year she said to the King—

"My dear, you ought to do something to distract your mind. It's unkinglike to sit and cry all day. Now, do make an effort; do something useful, if it's only opening a bazaar or laying a foundation stone."

"I am frightened of bazaars," said the King; "they are like bees—they buzz and worry; but foundation stones——" And after that he began to sit and think sometimes, without crying, and to make notes on the backs of old envelopes. So the Queen felt that she had not spoken quite in vain.

A month later the suggestion of foundation stones bore fruit.

The King floated a company, and Fortunatus Rex & Co. became almost at once the largest speculative builders in the world.

Perhaps you do not know what a speculative builder is. I'll tell you what the King and his Co. did, and then you will know.

They bought all the pretty woods and fields they could get and cut them up into squares, and grubbed up the trees and the grass and put streets there and lamp-posts and ugly little yellow brick houses, in the hopes that people would want to live in them. And curiously enough people did. So the King and his Co. made quite a lot of money.

It is curious that nearly all the great fortunes are made by turning beautiful things into ugly ones. Making beauty out of ugliness is very ill-paid work.

The ugly little streets crawled further and further out of the town, eating up the green country like greedy yellow caterpillars, but at the foot of the Clover Hill they had to stop. For the owner of Clover Hill would not sell any land at all—for any price that Fortunatus Rex & Co. could offer. In vain the solicitors of the Company called on the solicitors of the owner, wearing their best cloaks and swords and shields, and took them out to lunch and gave them nice things to eat and drink. Clover Hill was not for sale.

At last, however, a little old woman all in grey called at the Company's shining brass and mahogany offices and had a private interview with the King himself.

"I am the owner of Clover Hill," said she, "and you may build on all its acres except the seven at the top and the fifteen acres that go round that seven, and you must build me a high wall round the seven acres and another round the fifteen—of *red* brick, mind; none of your cheap yellow stuff—and you must make a brand new law that any one who steals my fruit is to be hanged from the tree he stole it from. That's all. What do you say?"

The King said "Yes," because since his trouble he cared for nothing but building, and his royal soul longed to see the green Clover Hill eaten up by yellow brick caterpillars with slate tops. He did not at all like building the two red brick walls, but he did it.

Now, the old woman wanted the walls and the acres to be this sort of shape—

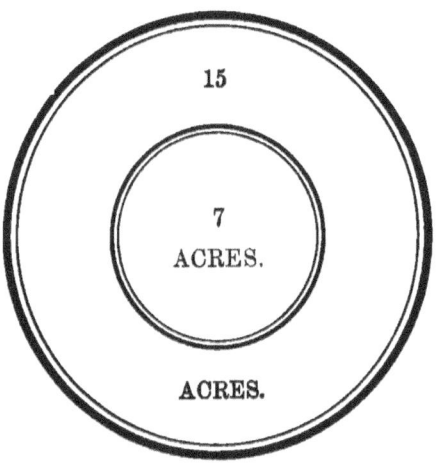

But it was such a bother getting the exact amount of ground into the two circles that all the surveyors tore out their hair by handfuls, and at last the King said, "Oh bother! Do it this way," and drew a plan on the back of an old Act of Parliament. So they did, and it was like this—

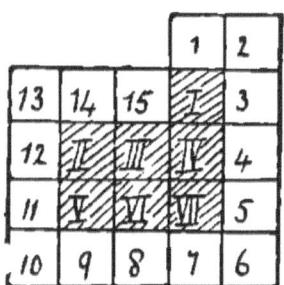

The old lady was very vexed when she found that there was only one wall between her orchard and the world, as you see was the case at the corner where the two 1's and the 15 meet; but the King said he couldn't afford to build it all over again and that she'd got her two walls as she had said.

So she had to put up with it. Only she insisted on the King's getting her a fierce bull-dog to fly at the throat of any one who should come over the wall at that weak point where the two 1's join on to the 15. So he got her a stout bull-dog whose name was Martha, and brought it himself in a jewelled leash.

"Martha will fly at any one who is not of kingly blood," said he. "Of course she wouldn't dream of biting a royal person; but, then, on the other hand, royal people don't rob orchards."

So the old woman had to be contented. She tied Martha up in the unprotected corner of her inner enclosure and then she planted little baby apple trees and had a house built and sat down in it and waited.

And the King was almost happy. The creepy, crawly yellow caterpillars ate up Clover Hill—all except the little green crown on the top, where the apple trees were and the two red brick walls and the little house and the old woman.

The poor Queen went on seeing to the jam and the pickles and the blanket washing and the spring cleaning, and every now and then she would say to her husband—

"Fortunatus, my love, do you *really* think Miss Fitzroy Robinson is trustworthy? Shall we ever see our Daisy again?"

And the King would rumple his fair hair with his hands till it stuck out like cheese straws under his crown, and answer—

"My dear, you must be patient; you know we had the very highest references."

Now one day the new yellow brick town the King had built had a delightful experience. Six handsome Princes on beautiful white horses came riding through the dusty little streets. The housings of their chargers shone with silver embroidery and gleaming glowing jewels, and their gold armour flashed so gloriously in the sun that all the little children clapped their hands, and the Princes' faces were so young and kind and handsome that all the old women said: "Bless their pretty hearts!"

Now, of course, you will not need to be told that these six Princes were looking for the six grown-up Princesses who had

15

been so happy at the Select Boarding Establishment. Their six Royal fathers, who lived many years' journey away on the other side of the world, and had not yet heard that the Princesses were mislaid, had given Miss Fitzroy Robinson's address to these Princes, and instructed them to marry the six Princesses without delay, and bring them home.

But when they got to the Select Boarding Establishment for the Daughters of Respectable Monarchs, the house was closed, and a card was in the window, saying that this desirable villa residence was to be let on moderate terms, furnished or otherwise. The wax fruit under the glass shade still showed attractively through the dusty panes. The six Princes looked through the window by turns. They were charmed with the furniture, and the refining touch of a woman's hand drew them like a magnet. They took the house, but they had their meals at the Palace by the King's special invitation.

King Fortunatus told the Princes the dreadful story of the disappearance of the entire Select School; and each Prince swore by his sword-hilt and his honour that he would find out the particular Princess that he was to marry, or perish in the attempt. For, of course, each Prince was to marry one Princess, mentioned by name in his instructions, and not one of the others.

The first night that the Princes spent in the furnished house passed quietly enough, so did the second and the third and the fourth, fifth and sixth, but on the seventh night, as the Princes sat playing spilikins in the schoolroom, they suddenly heard a voice that was not any of theirs. It said, "Open up Africa!"

The Princes looked here, there, and everywhere—but they could see no one. They had not been brought up to the exploring trade, and could not have opened up Africa if they had wanted to.

"Or cut through the Isthmus of Panama," said the voice again.

Now, as it happened, none of the six Princes were engineers. They confessed as much.

"Cut up China, then!" said the voice, desperately.

"It's like the ghost of a Tory newspaper," said one of the Princes.

And then suddenly they knew that the voice came from one of the pair of globes which hung in frames at the end of the schoolroom. It was the terrestrial globe.

"I'm inside," said the voice; "I can't get out. Oh, cut the globe—anywhere—and let me out. But the African route is most convenient."

Prince Primus opened up Africa with his sword, and out tumbled half a Professor of Magic.

"My other half's in there," he said, pointing to the Celestial globe. "Let my legs out, do——"

But Prince Secundus said, "Not so fast," and Prince Tertius said, "Why were you shut up?"

"I was shut up for as pretty a bit of parlour-magic as ever you saw in all your born days," said the top half of the Professor of Magic.

"Oh, you were, were you?" said Prince Quartus; "well, your legs aren't coming out just yet. We want to engage a competent magician. You'll do."

"But I'm not all here," said the Professor.

"Quite enough of you," said Prince Quintus.

"Now look here," said Prince Sextus; "we want to find our six Princesses. We can give a very good guess as to how they were lost; but we'll let bygones be bygones. You tell us how to find them, and after our weddings we'll restore your legs to the light of day."

"This half of me feels so faint," said the half Professor of Magic.

"What are we to do?" said all the Princes, threateningly; "if you don't tell us, you shall never have a leg to stand on."

"Steal apples," said the half Professor, hoarsely, and fainted away.

They left him lying on the bare boards between the inkstained desks, and off they went to steal apples. But this was not so easy. Because Fortunatus Rex & Co. had built, and built, and built, and apples do not grow freely in those parts of the country which have been "opened up" by speculative builders.

So at last they asked the little Prince Denis where he went for apples when he wanted them. And Denis said—

"The old woman at the top of Clover Hill has apples in her seven acres, and in her fifteen acres, but there's a fierce bulldog in the seven acres, and I've stolen all the apples in the fifteen acres myself."

"We'll try the seven acres," said the Princes.

"Very well," said Denis; "You'll be hanged if you're caught. So, as I put you up to it, I'm coming too, and if you won't take me, I'll tell. So there!"

For Denis was a most honourable little Prince, and felt that you must not send others into danger unless you go yourself, and he would never have stolen apples if it had not been quite as dangerous as leading armies.

So the Princes had to agree, and the very next night Denis let himself down out of his window by a knotted rope made of all the stockings his mother had knitted for him, and the grown-up Princes were waiting under the window, and off they all went to the orchard on the top of Clover Hill.

They climbed the wall at the proper corner, and Martha, the bulldog, who was very wellbred, and knew a Prince when she saw one, wagged her kinked tail respectfully and wished them good luck.

The Princes stole over the dewy orchard grass and looked at tree after tree: there were no apples on any of them.

Only at last, in the very middle of the orchard there was a tree with a copper trunk and brass branches, and leaves of silver. And on it hung seven beautiful golden apples.

So each Prince took one of the golden apples, very quietly, and off they went, anxious to get back to the half-Professor of Magic, and learn what to do next. No one had any doubt as to the half-Professor having told the truth; for when your legs depend on your speaking the truth you will not willingly tell a falsehood.

They stole away as quietly as they could, each with a gold apple in his hand, but as they went Prince Denis could not resist his longing to take a bite out of his apple. He opened his mouth very wide so as to get a good bite, and the next moment he howled aloud, for the apple was as hard as stone, and the poor little boy had broken nearly all his first teeth.

He flung the apple away in a rage, and the next moment the old woman rushed out of her house. She screamed. Martha barked. Prince Denis howled. The whole town was aroused, and the six Princes were arrested, and taken under a strong guard to the Tower. Denis was let off, on the ground of his youth, and, besides, he had lost most of his teeth, which is a severe punishment, even for stealing apples.

The King sat in his Hall of Justice next morning, and the old woman and the Princes came before him. When the story had been told, he said—

"My dear fellows, I hope you'll excuse me—the laws of hospitality are strict—but business is business after all. I should not like to have any constitutional unpleasantness over a little thing like this; you must all be hanged to-morrow morning."

The Princes were extremely vexed, but they did not make a fuss. They asked to see Denis, and told him what to do.

So Denis went to the furnished house which had once been a Select Boarding Establishment for the Daughters of Respectable Monarchs. The door was locked, but Denis knew a way in, because his sister had told him all about it one holiday. He got up on the roof and walked down the schoolroom chimney.

There, on the schoolroom floor, lay half a Professor of Magic, struggling feebly, and uttering sad, faint squeals.

"What are we to do now?" said Denis.

"Steal apples," said the half-Professor in a weak whisper. "Do let my legs out. Slice up the Great Bear—or the Milky Way would be a good one for them to come out by."

But Denis knew better.

"Not till we get the lost Princesses," said he, "now, what's to be done?"

"Steal apples I tell you," said the half-Professor, crossly; "seven apples—there—seven kisses. Cut them down. Oh go along with you, do. Leave me to die, you heartless boy. I've got pins and needles in my legs."

Then off ran Denis to the Seven Acre Orchard at the top of Clover Hill, and there were the six Princes hanging to the apple-tree, and the hangman had gone home to his dinner, and there was no one else about. And the Princes were not dead.

Denis climbed up the tree and cut the Princes down with the penknife of the gardener's boy. (You will often find this penknife mentioned in your German exercises; now you know why so much fuss is made about it.)

The Princes fell to the ground, and when they recovered their wits Denis told them what he had done.

"Oh why did you cut us down?" said the Princes, "we were having such happy dreams."

"Well," said Denis, shutting up the penknife of the gardener's boy, "of all the ungrateful chaps!" And he turned his back and marched off. But they ran quickly after him and thanked him and told him how they had been dreaming of walking arm in arm with the most dear and lovely Princesses in the world.

"Well," said Denis, "it's no use dreaming about *them*. You've got your own registered Princesses to find, and the half-Professor says, 'Steal apples.'"

"There aren't any more to steal," said the Princes—but when they looked, there were the gold apples back on the tree just as before.

So once again they each picked one, Denis chose a different one this time. He thought it might be softer. The last time he had chosen the biggest apple—but now he took the littlest apple of all.

"Seven kisses!" he cried, and began to kiss the little gold apple.

Each Prince kissed the apple he held, till the sound of kisses was like the whisper of the evening wind in leafy trees. And, of course, at the seventh kiss each Prince found that he had in his hand not an apple, but the fingers of a lovely Princess. As for Denis, he had got his little sister Daisy, and he was so glad he promised at once to give her his guinea-pigs and his whole collection of foreign postage stamps.

"What is your name, dear and lovely lady?" asked Prince Primus.

"Sexta," said his Princess. And then it turned out that every single one of the Princes had picked the wrong apple, so that each one had a Princess who was not the one mentioned in his letter of instructions. Secundus had plucked the apple that held Quinta, and Tertius held Quarta, and so on—and everything was as criss-cross-crooked as it possibly could be.

And yet nobody wanted to change.

Then the old woman came out of her house and looked at them and chuckled, and she said—

"You must be contented with what you have."

"We *are*," said all twelve of them, "but what about our parents?"

"They must put up with your choice," said the old woman, "it's the common lot of parents."

"I think you ought to sort yourselves out properly," said Denis; "I'm the only one who's got his right Princess—because I wasn't greedy. I took the smallest."

The tallest Princess showed him a red mark on her arm, where his little teeth had been two nights before, and everybody laughed.

But the old woman said—

"They can't change, my dear. When a Prince has picked a gold apple that has a Princess in it, and has kissed it till she comes out, no other Princess will ever do for him, any more than any other Prince will ever do for her."

While she was speaking the old woman got younger and younger and younger, till as she spoke the last words she was quite young, not more than fifty-five. And it was Miss Fitzroy Robinson!

Her pupils stepped forward one by one with respectful curtsies, and she allowed them to kiss her on the cheek, just as if it was breaking-up day.

Then, all together, and very happily, they went down to the

furnished villa that had once been the Select School, and when the half-professor had promised on his honour as a Magician to give up Magic and take to a respectable trade, they took his legs out of the starry sphere, and gave them back to him; and he joined himself together, and went off full of earnest resolve to live and die an honest plumber.

"My talents won't be quite wasted," said he; "a little hanky-panky is useful in most trades."

When the King asked Miss Fitzroy Robinson to name her own reward for restoring the Princesses, she said—

"Make the land green again, your Majesty."

So Fortunatus Rex & Co. devoted themselves to pulling down and carting off the yellow streets they had built. And now the country there is almost as green and pretty as it was before Princess Daisy and the six parlour-boarders were turned into gold apples.

"It was very clever of dear Miss Fitzroy Robinson to shut up that Professor in those two globes," said the Queen; "it shows the advantage of having lessons from the best Masters."

"Yes," said the King, "I always say that you cannot go far wrong if you insist on the highest references!"